# DISNEY · PIXAR

## MOVIE THEATER STORYBOOK

Adapted by Tisha Hamilton

## CONTENTS

Toy Story . . . . . . . . . . . . . . . 4

Toy Story 2 . . . . . . . . . . . . . . 12

Reader's Digest
Children's Books

Pleasantville, New York • Montréal, Québec • Bath, United Kingdom

Disney · PIXAR

# TOY STORY

DISK 1

1

**W**oody the cowboy was Andy's favorite toy. When Andy played pretend, Woody was the sheriff who always saved the day. Today, Woody had captured the robber, One-Eyed Bart. It was a good day's work. Andy grabbed Woody by the arms and swung him in the air.

"It's party time, Woody," Andy said. Andy's family was moving soon. His mother had planned Andy's birthday party early so all his friends could come. Andy brought Woody downstairs to see the decorations.

Andy ran back upstairs and put Woody on his bed. As soon as Andy left the room, Woody sat up.

"Pull my string!" Woody exclaimed. "The birthday party's today?" Andy's other toys were coming to life, too. Woody used Mike to announce the news. As soon as they found out about the

2 birthday party, Andy's toys began to worry. What if Andy's birthday presents replaced them? Woody sent the Green Army Men downstairs to scout out the situation. Hiding in

3 a plant, a soldier used binoculars to see what Andy was opening and reported back to the toys.

Just as a Green Army Man was relaying a message about a

surprise gift, the radio fell. The toys heard Andy and his friends coming upstairs. They raced back to their places and became ordinary toys once again.

The kids thundered into Andy's room. "This is where the spaceship lands!" someone said, placing a box on the bed and pushing Woody off. Then the kids ran back downstairs to have some cake. Woody crawled out from under Andy's bed. All the toys gathered around to see what was now in Woody's old spot on Andy's bed. It was a fancy space ranger toy.

"Buzz Lightyear to the rescue!" the new toy exclaimed. Everyone ooh-ed and aah-ed when they saw his purple snap-out wings. Buzz thought he was a real space ranger. He told the other toys that he could fly.

It looked like Woody's days as Andy's favorite toy were over. Buzz Lightyear had replaced him.

**7** Woody missed being Andy's favorite toy.

One day, Woody heard a mean-sounding voice shouting "Yes!" outside. It was Sid, the boy next door. Woody used Lenny

**8** the binoculars to see what Sid was up to. He and Buzz watched as Sid blew up a Combat Carl action figure.

Then they heard Andy's mom. "You can take one toy to Pizza Planet," she told Andy. Woody wanted to be that toy in the worst way. He tried to use RC, the remote control car, to push Buzz off the dresser so Andy wouldn't see him. But, by mistake, Woody knocked Buzz out of the window instead.

When Andy couldn't find Buzz, he took Woody instead. Buzz crawled out of the bushes just in time to see Andy carrying Woody to the car. He grabbed the bumper as the car drove away.

DISK 2

9

10

11

"Oh, no," Woody said to himself. "What have I done?" When the car stopped for gas, Buzz climbed in. Buzz was angry. He and Woody got into a fight and they fell out of the car. The car drove away without them. Luckily, Woody and Buzz saw a Pizza Planet delivery truck and jumped in.

When they arrived at Pizza Planet, Buzz saw what he thought was a spaceship and hopped in. It was really a crane game full of green alien toys. While Buzz was inside, Woody tried to rescue him. Just then, Sid came along and put a coin into the

machine. He used the claw to grab Buzz and got Woody, too.

"Gotcha!" he yelled. When they got to Sid's house Woody got a first-hand demonstration how Sid treated his toys. The first thing he did was use a magnifying glass to burn a hole in Woody's forehead! Later, he planned to strap a rocket to Buzz's back and shoot him into the air. When Sid left his room, Woody and Buzz tried to escape. As they tiptoed down the hall, Buzz warned Woody to be quiet. Too late! Sid's dog, Scud, woke up and started chasing them.

Hiding in the family room, Buzz saw a Buzz Lightyear commercial on TV. Suddenly Buzz realized the truth—he wasn't a real space ranger after all. Even so, he made one last

12

attempt to fly. Sid's sister Hannah found a broken Buzz at the bottom of the stairs. She had dressed him up for a tea party with her other dolls when Woody rescued him.

**13**

That night, Woody planned a daring escape with the help of Sid's mutant toys. They had to get away, or Sid was going to light the rocket strapped to Buzz's back. The toys made their move the next morning. They distracted Sid so Woody and Buzz could run to Andy's house. But they were too late! It was moving day. Woody and Buzz arrived just as the car and moving van were driving away.

**14**

They ran after the van with Scud snapping at their heels. Woody grabbed a rope dangling from the van while Buzz fought off Scud. Woody opened the van and got RC, the remote control car. As RC went to pick up Buzz, Woody was knocked out of the van. RC picked him up, too, and they raced to catch the van. Just as they were about to reach the van, RC's batteries died. Luckily, Buzz was

**15** still wearing the rocket Sid had strapped to his back. Woody lit the fuse and all three toys flew into the air. RC landed right in the van. Woody and Buzz kept flying.

"Uh-oh," Woody said. "We're in trouble."

Buzz opened his purple wings and said, "Not

**16** today, we're not," as they sailed right over the van and into the open sunroof of Andy's car. Woody and Buzz were back with Andy. It was a great day after all for the two new best friends.

**Disney · PIXAR**

# TOY STORY 2

DISK 1

1

W̲oody and Buzz were the best of friends. They were both toys, and they both belonged to a boy named Andy. Woody was an old-fashioned cowboy doll. Buzz Lightyear was a new space ranger toy. Buzz even starred in his own video game. Rex the dinosaur liked to play the video game and pretend he was a space ranger, too.

It was a big day in Andy's room. Andy was going to Cowboy Camp, and he was taking Woody with him. Andy's dog, Buster, came to say good-bye to Woody.

"I'm going to miss you while I'm at Cowboy Camp," Woody told Buster as he rubbed the dog's nose.

Then Andy ran into his room. There was just enough time to play with his favorite toys one last time. "It's the unstoppable duo of Woody and Buzz!" he said, holding the toys close together. Andy didn't realize Woody's sleeve was caught in Buzz's arm. When he tried to pull Woody and Buzz apart,

2 Woody's arm tore!

3 Now Woody was in no shape to go with Andy. Andy's mother put Woody on the shelf. Woody sadly watched Andy leave for Cowboy Camp without him. Then something even more terrible happened. Andy's mom decided to have a yard sale.

All the toys were frightened. What if Andy's mom decided to sell them?

Up on the shelf, Woody found another broken toy—Wheezy the penguin. When Andy's mom came looking for yard-sale toys, she took Wheezy. Woody couldn't let Wheezy be sold. He whistled for Buster and climbed onto his back. "Okay, boy. To the yard sale!" Woody said.

At the yard sale, Woody found Wheezy and tucked him under Buster's collar. As they rode back to the house on Buster, Woody fell off. That's when Al saw him. Al owned a toy store and was a toy collector. He was also a thief. He knew Woody was a valuable toy. Al tried to hide Woody in a pile of other yard-sale stuff. "I'll give you fifty cents for all this junk," he said to Andy's mom.

"I'm sorry," she replied. "That's an old family toy."

She took Woody and put him in a safe place. But Al was willing to do anything to get Woody. As the toys in Andy's room watched from the window, Al stole Woody, stuffed him in his bag, and left.

Buzz wasn't about to let his best friend get stolen. As Al drove away, Buzz raced after him. Buzz grabbed the bumper of Al's car, but he couldn't hang on. As he fell, he noted the car's license plate, LZTYBRN.

Al took Woody back to his apartment. Then he put on a yellow chicken suit and left to make another TV commercial for the toy store. At Al's Toy Barn, you could get all the toys you could buy for a "buck, buck, buck."

While Al was gone, Woody looked around. Al had all kinds of things with Woody's picture on them. There were posters, a lamp, and even an old-fashioned record player. "Holy cow," Woody gasped.

A frisky toy horse raced up and took Woody for a ride. A cowgirl doll grabbed Woody and gave him a big hug. "Yee-hah!" she cried. "It's you! It's really you!"

Woody didn't know what she was talking about until she showed him an old TV show called *Woody's Roundup*. He learned that Bullseye was his horse, Jessie was the show's yodeling cowgirl, and he was the star of the show—the rootin'-tootinest cowboy in the West. The Prospector was another character on the show, and Al had a Prospector doll, too.

DISK 2

Back in Andy's room, the toys worked on a plan to rescue Woody. First, Etch A Sketch drew a picture of the man who stole Woody. Then Buzz typed the license plate letters into Mr. Spell. "LZTYBRN," said Mr. Spell, "Al's Toy Barn!" Quickly, they turned on the TV. When the commercial came on, Etch A Sketch copied the map with directions to the store.

Buzz, Slinky Dog, Rex, Hamm, and Mr. Potato Head formed a rescue team. One at a time, Slinky Dog carefully lowered them out the window and down to the ground. It was very dangerous, but the toys were brave. They were determined to save Woody.

When Al came home, he grabbed Woody off the shelf. But as he did, a thread from Woody's torn arm

**11** got caught and began to unravel. The next thing Al knew, Woody's arm had come off! Al was horrified.

**12** Al called the Cleaner. He came to clean and repair Woody. "He's for display only," he told Al when he was done. Al didn't care. He didn't steal Woody to play with him. He was planning to sell Woody and all the other *Woody's Roundup* toys to a museum!

**13** Al didn't know it, but Andy's toys were getting closer. Hiding under traffic cones, they crossed a busy street to get to Al's Toy Barn. Inside the store, they found a toy car, and searched the aisles for Woody. Woody wasn't there—and that meant he must be at Al's apartment.

Luckily, Al came into the store a short time later. The toys sneaked into his bag as he was leaving. When the toys finally got to Al's apartment, they tried to rescue Woody from Bullseye and Jessie, who were only having fun tickling him.

"Wait a minute," Woody said. "These are my new friends." Then he explained to Buzz and the other toys that he had decided to stay with his *Woody's Roundup* gang. Woody felt bad. He knew he would miss Andy and all his old friends, but he just couldn't leave Jessie and Bullseye. Without Woody, Al would just pack them back in the crates they'd been trapped in for years.

"Andy needs you, too," Buzz reminded Woody.

After his friends left, Woody had a great idea. He would go back to Andy after all, but he would take Jessie and Bullseye with him. The Prospector

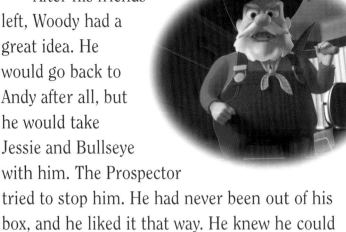

tried to stop him. He had never been out of his box, and he liked it that way. He knew he could only get to the museum if they all went.

Then Al came home. He packed all the *Woody's Roundup* toys into a suitcase, and took them to the airport. Woody tried to escape, but the Prospector pulled him back.

Woody's friends were not about to give up on Woody. They followed Al to the airport. Once again, it was Andy's toys to the rescue.

15

Buzz, Slinky Dog, Rex, Hamm, and Mr. Potato Head fought off the Prospector to rescue Woody and Bullseye, but Jessie was still trapped in the suitcase! Woody was determined to save her, and he raced after the suitcase.

Just as the plane was about to take off with the suitcase aboard, Woody freed her. They were dangling dangerously from the plane when Buzz rode up on Bullseye.

"Buzz Lightyear to the rescue!" he shouted as he caught Woody and Jessie. Woody was glad to be going back home to Andy's house, and especially glad that now all his best friends were together—Jessie, Bullseye, and Buzz.

Andy came home from Cowboy Camp that night, and there was a surprise waiting for him. All his toys lined up to welcome him back. There were even two new toys, Jessie and Bullseye. Andy was so excited. "Oh, wow! New toys!" he exclaimed.

Woody and Buzz were back together again after a great adventure. Woody couldn't have been happier. "I'll have old Buzz to keep me company—for infinity and beyond!" Woody declared.